Foxwood Ta[les]

presents the story of
Harvey
Rue and Willy in....

For Amanda, Christopher, Catherine
and Robert Jr.

A Beaver Book
Published by Arrow Books Limited
62–5 Chandos Place, London WC2N 4NW
An imprint of Century Hutchinson Ltd
London Melbourne Sydney Auckland
Johannesburg and agencies throughout the world

First published by André Deutsch 1985
Beaver edition 1986
Text © Cynthia Paterson 1985
Illustrations © Brian Paterson 1985
All rights reserved

Made and printed in Great Britain
by Scotprint, Musselburgh

ISBN 0 09 946270 2

Robbery at Foxwood

Open
Soon.

Written and Illustrated by
Cynthia & Brian Paterson

BEAVER BOOKS

The village clock struck 5.30. Mr Gruffey was just crossing the
shop to lock up when Mrs Hedgehog popped her head round the door.

'Do you know what the time is?' he said angrily.

'I haven't time to worry about the time,' she said, 'I have more important things to do.'

Mrs Hedgehog helped herself as Mr Gruffey drummed his fingers impatiently on the counter muttering about late comers and muddy floors and adding up the takings.

'And there's another thing,' he said suddenly, 'your Willy's outside playing cricket with that Harvey mouse and Rue rabbit; twice already their ball has hit my shop and if they do any damage you can be sure it will be on your bill at the end of the week.'

'Don't worry, I'll tell Willy to be careful,' said Mrs Hedgehog, as she popped the last item into her basket and hurried off home to make the tea.

Crash!

'Crikey! We've broken old Gruffey's window,' shouted Rue.
Mr Gruffey came charging from his shop shaking his fist with
rage. 'You wicked boys, now look what you've done,' he bellowed.
If I've told you once I've told you a thousand times. This time you'll
have to pay for it. Now off home with you, your mothers shall know
about this first thing in the morning.'

Mr Gruffey went back to inspect the damage. 'It's too late to get it repaired tonight,' he muttered, as he locked up the shop and went home. 'I'll have to leave it till tomorrow.'

Harvey was late getting home and his mother was cross. He toyed with his supper but just couldn't eat.

'It's your own fault if your watercress soup's cold,' said his mother, thinking he didn't like it.

'It's not that, Mum,' Harvey burst out. 'We've broken Mr Gruffey's shop window playing cricket, and he's very angry.'

'Oh, Harvey, how could you? We shall have to pay for it, you know. If only you'd think before you did such stupid things you might not cause so much trouble.'

Harvey felt very ashamed as his mother washed him and helped him into his clean, neatly pressed pyjamas.

'Well what's done is done,' she said as she kissed him goodnight. 'It might be a good idea if you visit Mr Gruffey in the morning to sort out a way of repaying him for the damage.'

'What a super idea, Mum,' he said, feeling better already.

Harvey awoke early, and on his way past the shop to Mr Gruffey's cottage, noticed the door was open.

He peered inside, expecting to see Mr Gruffey, but instead saw only rows of empty shelves and boxes.

'Robbers,' he gasped, and ran off to tell Mr Gruffey the dreadful news.

Mr Gruffey had just climbed out of bed when he heard a loud knocking at the front door. 'Go away,' he shouted. 'I don't open till nine o'clock.'

The knocking went on. 'Mr Gruffey, come quickly,' called a voice.

He opened the front door – just a little – and peered through.

'Mr Gruffey, your shop's been robbed,' panted Harvey.

'Go away, boy,' said Mr Gruffey angrily 'I'm tired of your silly jokes.'

'But it's true,' said Harvey. 'Please come.'

Mr Gruffey grabbed his coat, slammed the door behind him and ran after Harvey to the shop.

Mr Gruffey stood in the doorway. He stared at the empty shop, unable to believe his eyes.

'How did they get in?' he muttered.

Willy and Rue had heard Harvey calling Mr Gruffey and came to see what had happened. Harvey looked at them. 'It's our fault,' he said miserably. 'They must have got in through the broken window.'

Mr Gruffey said nothing. He was too upset even to be cross.

'We'll find the robbers,' said Harvey.

'We'll get everything back,' said Willy.

'Perhaps they dropped some of the stuff,' said Rue. 'Let's look.'

They searched in front of the shop for clues.

'I can't see anything here,' said Willy, and he went round to the back, which was hidden from the road. The store room window was open and there were footprints, much bigger than his own, in the short grass. Investigating further he found empty toffee papers, then he spotted cart tracks leading away from the open window.

'Look what I've found,' he shouted, and the others hurried to see.

'Well done,' said Rue. 'Look, the footprints and cart tracks lead away into the woods. Let's follow them.'

The robbers had had a good start on Harvey, Rue and Willy, but they followed the tracks bravely through the woods and fields near the village getting more and more tired.

'I can't go on,' said Willy. 'I'm tired, cold and hungry, and my feet are sore. Why don't we go home and start again from here in the morning?'

'Don't be silly,' said Rue. 'We'd have to get all the way back here before we could start again from here.' He gave Willy a helpful shove up the hill. 'We can't go back now, but if we go on we may find some shelter and a place to rest for the night.'

They followed the fading tracks for
another mile down a steep hill.
The road on the opposite side of
the valley stretched before
them like a ribbon in
the moonlight.

They passed a
rather creepy
looking cottage
and crossed a
ricketty old
bridge, leaving
the gurgling
stream behind
them as they
made their
way up the
winding lane
on the other
side of the valley.

Halfway up the
hill Harvey spotted
a scarecrow at the top.

'Scarecrows see every-
thing,' he said. 'If the
robbers have passed this way
he will tell us which way they went.'

'If he doesn't,' said Willy, 'I'm going to stop with him for the night. I'm too tired to walk another step.' The old scarecrow was dozing in the moonlight, but he awoke with a start as they approached. 'Who's there?' he shouted. 'Can you help us?' said Harvey. 'Mr Gruffey's been robbed of all his groceries and we're looking for the thieves. Have you seen anyone suspicious?' 'Mmm,' said the scarecrow thoughtfully. 'There are some tinkers camping over at Robbers' Copse. When they went by they had a loaded cart with them, so they might be the one's you're after.'

Harvey Rue and Willy thanked the scarecrow for his help, waved goodbye and went their weary way along the lane. Ahead they saw a small flickering light.

'Look,' said Willy suddenly, 'another empty toffee paper; we're still on the right track.'

'Wait here,' said Harvey, 'I'll sneak up to the light and have a look.'

He crawled through the undergrowth, taking care not to snap anything in his path. When he reached the tinkers' camp he peered through a small gap in the hedge.

There, sitting around a glowing camp fire, were three of the biggest, meanest looking weasels Harvey had ever seen. They were laughing and joking and their mouths were full of sticky toffee. Beside them stood Mr Gruffey's handcart piled high with groceries, sweets and vegetables. Harvey grinned.

'It looks as if everything's still here,' he muttered. 'They can't have had time to sell anything.'

Harvey still couldn't believe his luck as he ran back to tell the others.

'Oh dear,' said Willy, 'will we have to fight them?'

'They're too big to fight,' said Harvey, 'we'll have to use a cunning plan to get the groceries back.'

All three were racking their brains when a party of glow-worms came by. 'Good evening,' said the leader. 'What are you doing out so late?'

As Rue was telling the glow-worms all about the robbery and the chase, Harvey suddenly shouted. 'I've got it.'

'Got what?' asked Willy.

'The cunning plan, of course,' answered Harvey. 'Listen. Rue you're the fastest, run back to the scarecrow and ask if we can borrow his turnip head for an hour or two. Willy and I will cut a good long stick from the hedge; we'll tie the turnip on it and . . .'

'I know,' interrupted a glow-worm, 'you want us to climb inside and turn it into a lantern.'

'Precisely,' said Harvey.

'I've got it,' said Willy, 'we pretend we're ghosts and scare them off.'

Everything went according to plan. Rue came back with the turnip head, Willy and Harvey tied it tightly to the stick and the glow-worms climbed inside and glowed.

The three friends crept silently up to the robbers' camp and waited patiently until the weasels were sleepy and their camp fire had burned down.

'Now,' whispered Harvey. 'Now or never.' They lifted the head above the hedge and waved it to and fro, making scarey moans and wails and other ghostly noises.

The weasels were terrified. They didn't even stop to think about the cart, they just ran for their lives.

'We've done it.' shouted Harvey. 'Hurray. They've gone.'

Willy and Rue gently lifted the glow-worms out of the scarecrow's head and thanked them for their help.

'Don't mention it,' said the glow-worms, 'we've enjoyed ourselves,' and they crawled off into the night.

Harvey and Rue looked at the handcart. 'We need some rope,' said Harvey, 'or the whole lot will fall off.' They found a length of rope by the camp and secured the goods.

'Do hurry up,' cried Willy, 'the weasels might come back and chase us.'

'Easier said than done,' snapped Harvey. 'We might get on better with some help.' Then he looked at Willy, almost asleep on his feet. 'Come on,' he said more kindly, 'hop on top and we'll give you a lift.'

The moon peeped out from behind the clouds and guided them homewards. As they passed the scarecrow they gave him back his head and thanked him warmly for his help. 'We wouldn't have managed without you,' said Harvey.

'Don't thank me,' said the scarecrow. 'I'm glad to have been of use. Life's pretty dull round here, you know.'

Back in the village Mrs Mouse,
Mrs Rabbit and Mrs Hedgehog were
becoming very worried and the more they
worried the crosser they became with Mr Gruffey.

Poor Mr Gruffey, he was often grumpy and bad tempered,
but he had a kind heart underneath and he too was very concerned
when Harvey, Rue and Willy had not come home by nightfall.

'We must go and look for them,' he declared.

It took a long time, but just before dawn a search party
carrying lanterns, blankets and flasks of hot tea was ready to go.

Mr Gruffey lead the way on the long search through the shadowy woodland. As they reached the edge of the big wood he stopped suddenly. Three mysterious shapes were creaking and rumbling towards them.

'Who's there?' he shouted. 'Stop or I'll . . .'

'It's us,' cried Harvey. 'We're back and we've got Mr Gruffey's stuff. All of it.'

Everyone rushed to greet them.

Harvey ran into his mother's arms and she wrapped him in the warm folds of her cloak. Rue and his mother hugged and squeezed each other tightly as Mr Gruffey lifted Willy out of the handcart and handed him over to his mother. It had been a long hard journey. Sleepy and exhausted the friends returned home and Mrs Mouse whispered to Harvey that she had a nice bowl of *hot* watercress soup waiting for him.

Mr Gruffey was so happy that Harvey, Rue and Willy were safe and he could open a fully stocked shop in the morning, that he decided there and then, to give a party for the whole village.

The next morning Mr Gruffey rummaged around in his old store chest.

'Found it,' he said, producing a piece of chicken wire. Then, picking up some nails and a hammer he nailed it over the window in the door. 'Now they can play cricket all day long without breaking another window,' he said happily.

Everyone enjoyed the party. Harvey, Rue and Willy were treated like heroes and Mr Gruffey made an opening speech after which he presented them with medals for bravery.

They were shiny gold on the outside and inside full of the loveliest chocolate you have ever tasted.